P9-DMV-925

WITHDRAWN

A Note to Parents and Caregivers:

Read-it! Readers are for children who are just starting on the amazing road to reading. These beautiful books support both the acquisition of reading skills and the love of books.

The RED LEVEL presents familiar topics using common words and repeating sentence patterns.

The BLUE LEVEL presents new ideas using a larger vocabulary and varied sentence structure.

The YELLOW LEVEL presents more challenging ideas, a broad vocabulary, and wide variety in sentence structure.

The GREEN LEVEL presents more complex ideas, an extended vocabulary range, and expanded language structures.

When sharing a book with your child, read in short stretches, pausing often to talk about the pictures. Have your child turn the pages and point to the pictures and familiar words. And be sure to reread favorite stories or parts of stories.

There is no right or wrong way to share books with children. Find time to read with your child, and pass on the legacy of literacy.

Adria F. Klein, Ph.D.
Professor Emeritus
California State University
San Bernardino, California

Managing Editor: Bob Temple
Creative Director: Terri Foley
Editor: Brenda Haugen
Editorial Adviser: Andrea Cascardi
Copy Editor: Laurie Kahn
Designer: Melissa Voda
Page production: The Design Lab
The illustrations in this book were prepared digitally.

Picture Window Books
5115 Excelsior Boulevard
Suite 232
Minneapolis, MN 55416
1-877-845-8392
www.picturewindowbooks.com

Printed in the United States of America.

Library of Congress Cataloging-in-Publication Data
Blair, Eric.
The crow and the pitcher : a retelling of Aesop's fable / by Eric Blair ; illustrated by Dianne
Silverman.
p. cm. — (Read-it! readers)
Summary: When a thirsty crow cannot drink from a pitcher because the water level is too
low, she uses her ingenuity to solve the problem.
ISBN 1-4048-0322-X (Reinforced Library Binding)
[1. Fables. 2. Folklore.] I. Aesop. II. Silverman, Dianne, ill. III.
Title. IV. Series.
PZ8.2.B595 Cr 2004
398.2—dc22
                                                                    2003016676

Read-it! Readers
Yellow Level

The Crow and the Pitcher

A Retelling of Aesop's Fable
By Eric Blair

Illustrated by Dianne Silverman

Content Adviser:
Kathy Baxter, M.A.
Former Coordinator of Children's Services
Anoka County (Minnesota) Library

Reading Advisers:
Adria F. Klein, Ph.D.
Professor Emeritus, California State University
San Bernardino, California

Susan Kesselring, M.A.
Literacy Educator
Rosemount-Apple Valley-Eagan (Minnesota) School District

Picture Window Books
Minneapolis, Minnesota

What Is a Fable?

A fable is a story that teaches a lesson. In some fables, animals may talk and act the way people do. A Greek slave named Aesop created some of the world's favorite fables. Aesop's fables have been enjoyed by readers for more than 2,000 years.

There was once a thirsty crow.

She had flown a long way
looking for water.

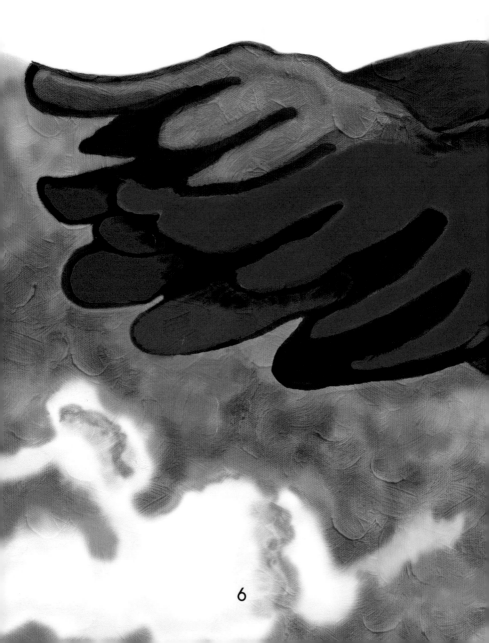

The thirsty crow saw a pitcher of water and flew down to drink.

The pitcher had only a little water left at the bottom.

The crow put her beak
into the pitcher. The water
was so low she couldn't
reach it.

But I must have water to drink.

I can't fly any farther, thought the crow.

11

I know. I'll tip the pitcher over, she thought.

The thirsty crow beat the pitcher with her wings, but she wasn't strong enough to tip it.

13

Maybe I can break the pitcher.
Then the water will flow,
thought the crow.

She backed away to get a flying start.

With all her might, the thirsty crow
flew at the pitcher.

She struck it with her pointed beak and claws, but the tired crow wasn't strong enough to break the pitcher.

Just as she was about to give up, the crow had another idea. She dropped a pebble into the pitcher. The water rose a little.

She dropped another and
another. With each pebble,
the water level rose more.

19

Soon the water reached the brim.
The crow drank until she was
no longer thirsty.

The crow was pleased with herself.
By refusing to give up, she had solved
her difficult problem.

Levels for *Read-it!* Readers

Read-it! Readers help children practice early reading skills
with brightly illustrated stories.

 Red Level: Familiar topics with frequently used words and repeating patterns.

 Blue Level: New ideas with a larger vocabulary and a variety of language structures.

The Donkey in the Lion's Skin, by Eric Blair 1-4048-0320-3

The Goose that Laid the Golden Egg, by Mark White 1-4048-0219-3

 Yellow Level: Challenging ideas with an expanded vocabulary and a wide variety of sentences.

The Ant and the Grasshopper, by Mark White 1-4048-0217-7

The Boy Who Cried Wolf, by Eric Blair 1-4048-0319-X

The Country Mouse and the City Mouse, by Eric Blair 1-4048-0318-1

The Crow and the Pitcher, by Eric Blair 1-4048-0322-X

The Dog and the Wolf, by Eric Blair 1-4048-0323-8

The Fox and the Grapes, by Mark White 1-4048-0218-5

The Tortoise and the Hare, by Mark White 1-4048-0215-0

The Wolf in Sheep's Clothing, by Mark White 1-4048-0220-7

 Green Level: More complex ideas with an extended vocabulary range and expanded language structures.

Belling the Cat, by Eric Blair 1-4048-0321-1

The Lion and the Mouse, by Mark White 1-4048-0216-9

23